Read more Haggis and Tank adventures!

Howl at the Moon

by **Jessica Young**
illustrated by **James Burks**

SCHOLASTIC INC.

For Sharon and Philip, and everyone
who loves to howl -JY

For Maddie—Every day is a new beginning -JB

Text copyright © 2017 by Jessica Young
Illustrations copyright © 2017 by James Burks

Library of Congress Cataloging-in-Publication Data

Names: Young, Jessica (Jessica E.), author. | Burks, James (James R.), illustrator. | Young, Jessica (Jessica E.). Haggis and Tank unleashed ; 3. Title: Howl at the moon / by Jessica Young ; illustrated by James Burks. Description: First edition. | New York, NY : Branches/Scholastic Inc., 2017. | Series: Haggis and Tank unleashed ; 3 | Summary: In this adventure Tank the Great Dane's active imagination takes her and Haggis the Scotty on a airplane trip to Scotland, where they visit a castle, enjoy high tea—and get chased by a werewolf. Identifiers: LCCN 2016040569| ISBN 9781338045253 (pbk.) | ISBN 9781338045260 (hardcover) Subjects: LCSH: Great Dane—Juvenile fiction. | Scottish terrier—Juvenile fiction. | Imagination—Juvenile fiction. | Werewolves—Juvenile fiction. | Scotland—Juvenile fiction. | CYAC: Great Dane—Fiction. | Scottish terrier—Fiction. | Dogs—Fiction. | Imagination—Fiction. | Werewolves—Fiction. | Scotland—Fiction. Classification: LCC PZ7.Y8657 Ho 2017 | DDC 813.6 [E] —dc23
LC record available at https://lccn.loc.gov/2016040569

ISBN 978-1-338-04526-0 (hardcover) / ISBN 978-1-338-04525-3 (paperback)

10 9 8 7   20 21

Printed in China   62
First edition, May 2017
Edited by Katie Carella
Book design by Cheung Tai

TABLE OF CONTENTS

CHAPTER ONE
CASTLE CALLING

Haggis was doing his afternoon stretches.

He was enjoying some peace and quiet.

Tank was practicing her howl.

Tank read the book.

The book gave her an idea.

Haggis did not want to fly.

Haggis packed his bag.

Tank got the plane ready.

Haggis climbed in.

Haggis tried to escape.

But it was too late.

Haggis and Tank zoomed down the runway.

ZZZOOOOOO

They were flying!

CHAPTER TWO

FOGGY DOGGIES

Tank loved being a pilot.

13

Flying made Tank hungry.

Is it just me, or does that cloud look like a cheeseburger?

She served some snacks.

Would you like a peanut butter pizza puff?

TANK! Just fly the plane!

crunch *crunch*

Tank flew . . .

and flew . . .

and flew.

15

Suddenly, the clouds turned dark.

The engine started to sputter.

It was a bumpy landing.

Tank jumped out of the plane.

Haggis climbed down the ladder.

The soggy dogs slogged through the foggy, froggy bog.

I hope we find the castle soon. I'm chilly.

Mmm . . . chili!

Haggis checked the map.

Just then, Tank spotted something in the distance.

Haggis and Tank crossed the
bridge to the castle.

FOGGY
BOTTOM
CASTLE

Tank knocked on the castle door.

The door creaked open.

CHAPTER THREE

PRINCE PRINTS

Haggis and Tank stepped inside the castle.

Haggis and Tank peeked into the dining room.

The table was set for tea.

It's teatime, Haggis!

High tea in a real Scottish castle! This is a dream come true!

Haggis poured the tea.

Haggis was happy.

A toast to Scotland! And to high tea!

Hi, tea!

slurp
slurp

Bye, tea!

Tank was hungry.

I need a snack. Let's try some scones, Haggis.

I guess we could try one. Oh, dear—someone spilled the jam.

Mmm, strawberry!

Tank helped herself.

Just then, Haggis spotted a picture on the wall.

Haggis and Tank went to find the prince.

They found the library.

Tank picked up a book.

Tank read the cover.

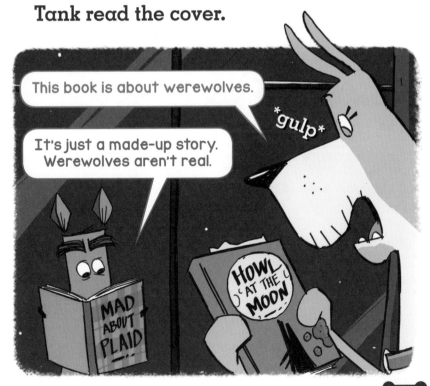

Tank opened the book. There was a piece of paper inside.

CHAPTER FOUR
WHO HOO-HOOED?

Tank was worried about the werewolf.

Maybe we should go home.

Tank, there's no such thing as a werewolf. Besides, we're safe inside the castle.

I hope Prince Pants-A-Lot is okay.
I'm sure he'll be back soon. Why don't you find a funny book to read?

Tank looked for a new book.

She found a surprise.

Haggis tried to play the bagpipes.

But he couldn't make a noise.

GASP
PANT
PANT

You just need practice.

I just need a good night's sleep.

43

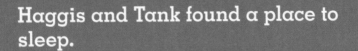
Haggis and Tank found a place to sleep.

Haggis, look! That knight will protect us from the werewolf!

That's just a suit of armor. I bet a knight wore it to war.

They climbed into bed.

Haggis turned out the light.

Then Haggis and Tank heard a strange sound.

Yoo-hoo, Haggis! Did you hoo-hoo?

I bark. I do not hoo-hoo.

If _you_ did not hoo-hoo, then _who_ hoo-hoo-ed?

What if it's that horrible werewolf?

I have an idea— why don't you go find out?

HOO-HOO!

I will!

Tank tiptoed toward the noise.

HOO-HOOO!

She tripped.

CLATTER!

CRASH! CLANG!

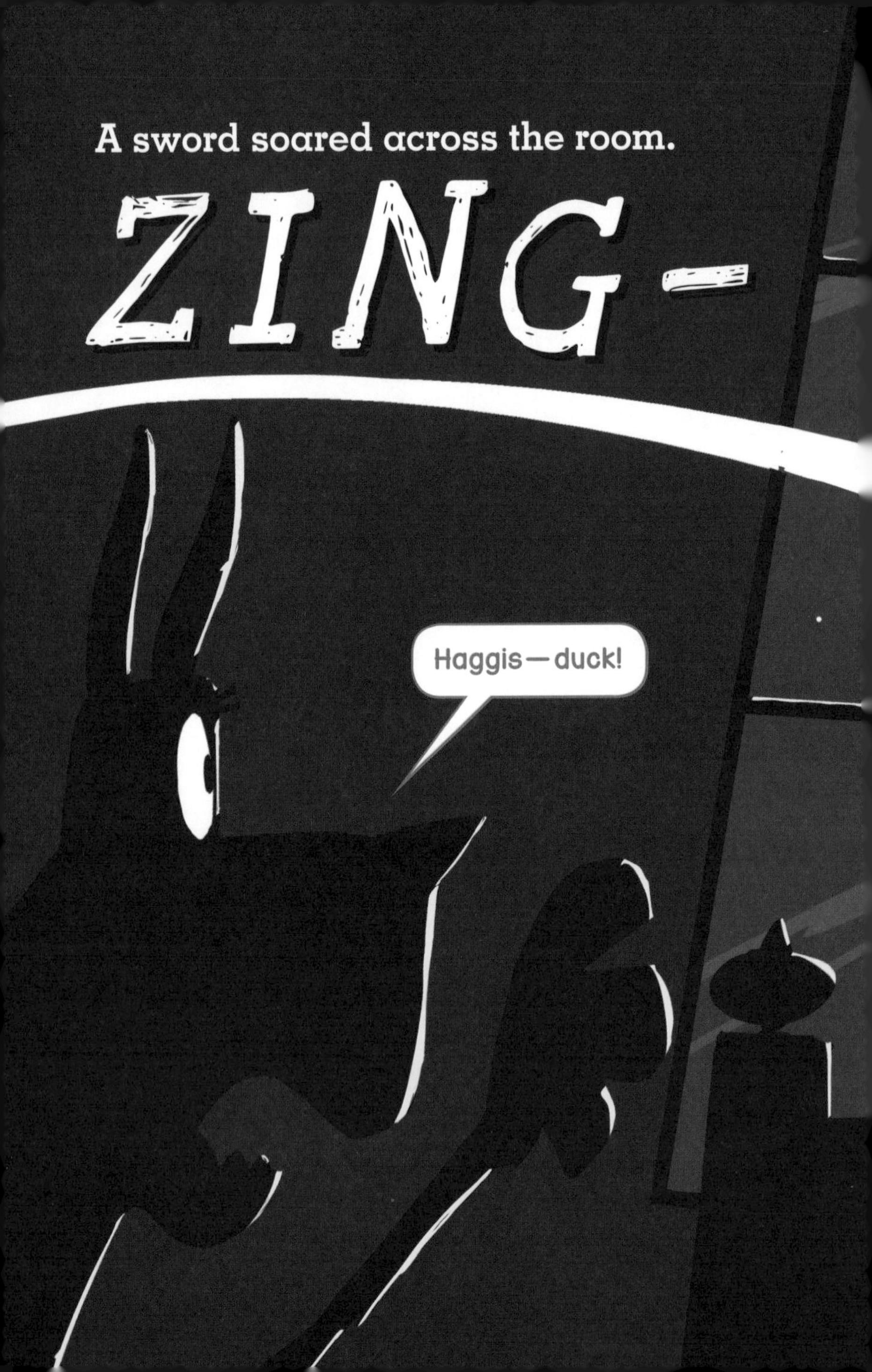
A sword soared across the room.
ZING-
Haggis—duck!

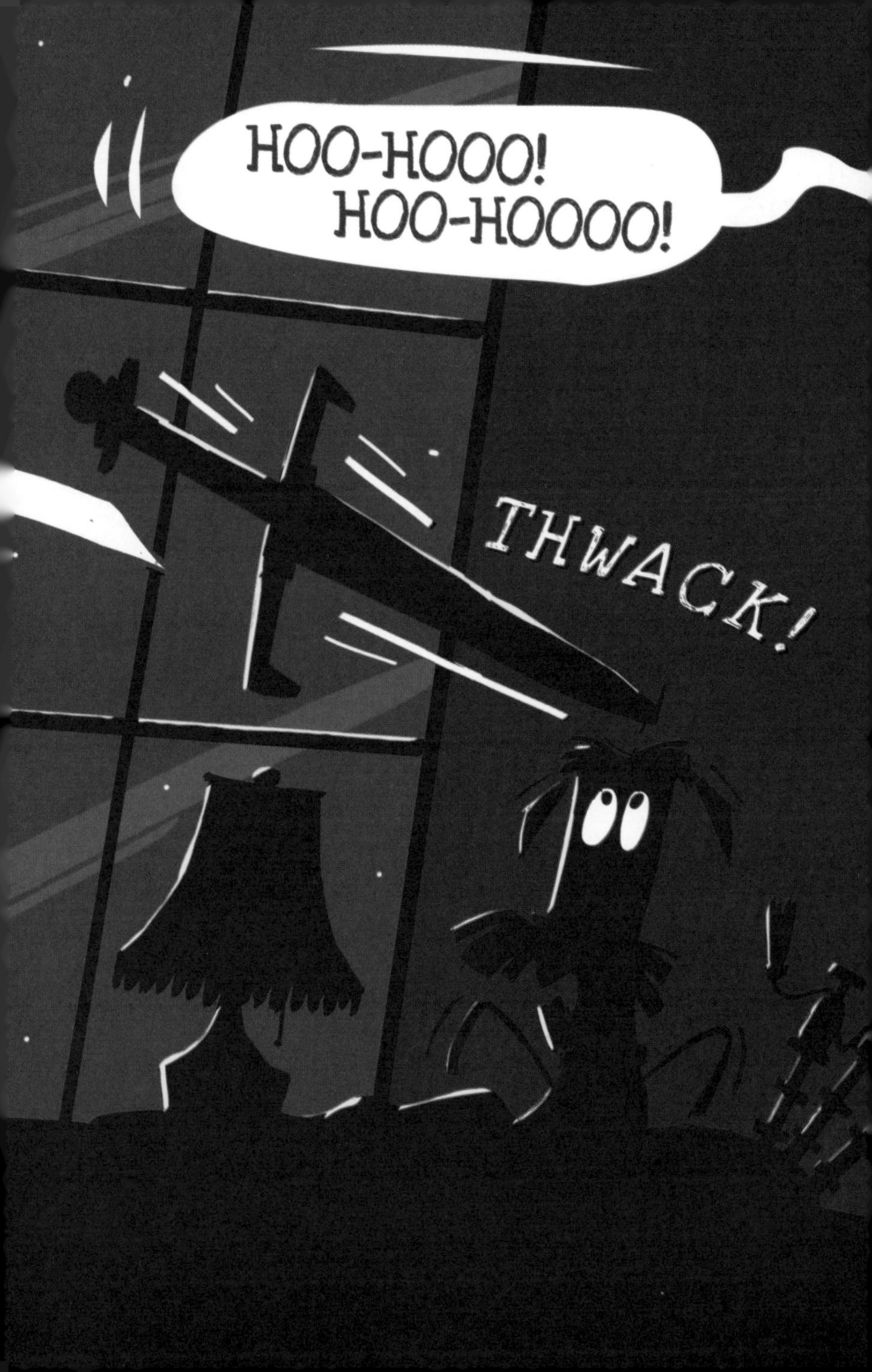
HOO-HOOO! HOO-HOOOO!
THWACK!

Haggis turned on the light.

HOO-HOOOO!

Aw, you're not horrible—you're adorable!

Haggis and Tank climbed back into bed.

Mystery solved. Good night, Tank.

Night-night, Haggis. Night-night, knight. Night-night, owl.

Soon they heard a different sound.

CHAPTER FIVE
WHERE'S THE WEREWOLF?

The howling got louder.

Haggis and Tank ran to the window.

They saw the werewolf.

The werewolf saw them.

PRINCE PANTS-A-LOT!

pant

pant

pant

55

Tank—duck in there!

There's no duck in here!

This way!

That way!

That way!

This way!

CRASH!

Haggis and Tank raced through the maze.

The werewolf was right behind them.

A-WOOOOOOO!

Hurry, Haggis!

Dead end!

Haggis and Tank dashed down a different path.

Finally, they found a way out.

Tank spotted a boat in the moat.

Haggis and Tank jumped into the boat.

Tank sat on the bagpipes and rowed.

Haggis played the bagpipes.

CHAPTER SIX

HOW TO HOWL

Suddenly, Tank stopped rowing.

The moon shone down like a great, glowing ball of cheese.

It gave her a funny feeling.

She threw back her head.

Then she howled.

The werewolf ran back to the castle.

Wow, Tank! Your howl scared him away!

Woof.

Did you hear that were-<u>woof</u>? He sounds sad.

Wait a minute—

we have his bagpipes!

Property of: Prince Pants-A-Lot

That's <u>why</u> he was chasing us! We'd better give them back.

Tank threw the bagpipes to the werewolf.

FLING!

WOO! A-WOOOOO!

Thanks for letting us borrow your bagpipes!

Haggis and Tank were back in their own backyard.

71

Jessica Young

grew up in Ontario, Canada. She has never played the bagpipes, but she loves playing with words and dreaming up stories! Her other books include SPY GUY THE NOT-SO-SECRET AGENT, the FINLEY FLOWERS series, and the award-winning MY BLUE IS HAPPY. HAGGIS AND TANK UNLEASHED is her first early chapter book series.

James Burks

lives in sunny California. Even though he is not a dog, James enjoys chasing squirrels, getting belly rubs, and running around the dog park. His other books include the award-winning GABBY AND GATOR, BEEP AND BAH, and the BIRD AND SQUIRREL graphic novel series.

How much do you know about Howl at the Moon?

Look at pages 48-49. Use the words and pictures to figure out the meanings of *sword* and *soared*.

When Haggis and Tank first enter the castle, why does Tank think someone is home? What does she hear?

Look at page 33. Why is the prince's name funny? What is the prince wearing in the painting?

Why does the werewolf chase Haggis and Tank? What does he want that they have? Reread pages 66-67 for clues.

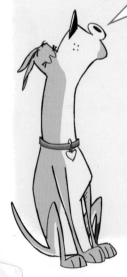

Haggis has always wanted to visit Scotland and to play the bagpipes. Where do you want to take a trip? What would you do there? Use words and pictures to explain.